2nd Grade
Unit 2

Maine

mpshire

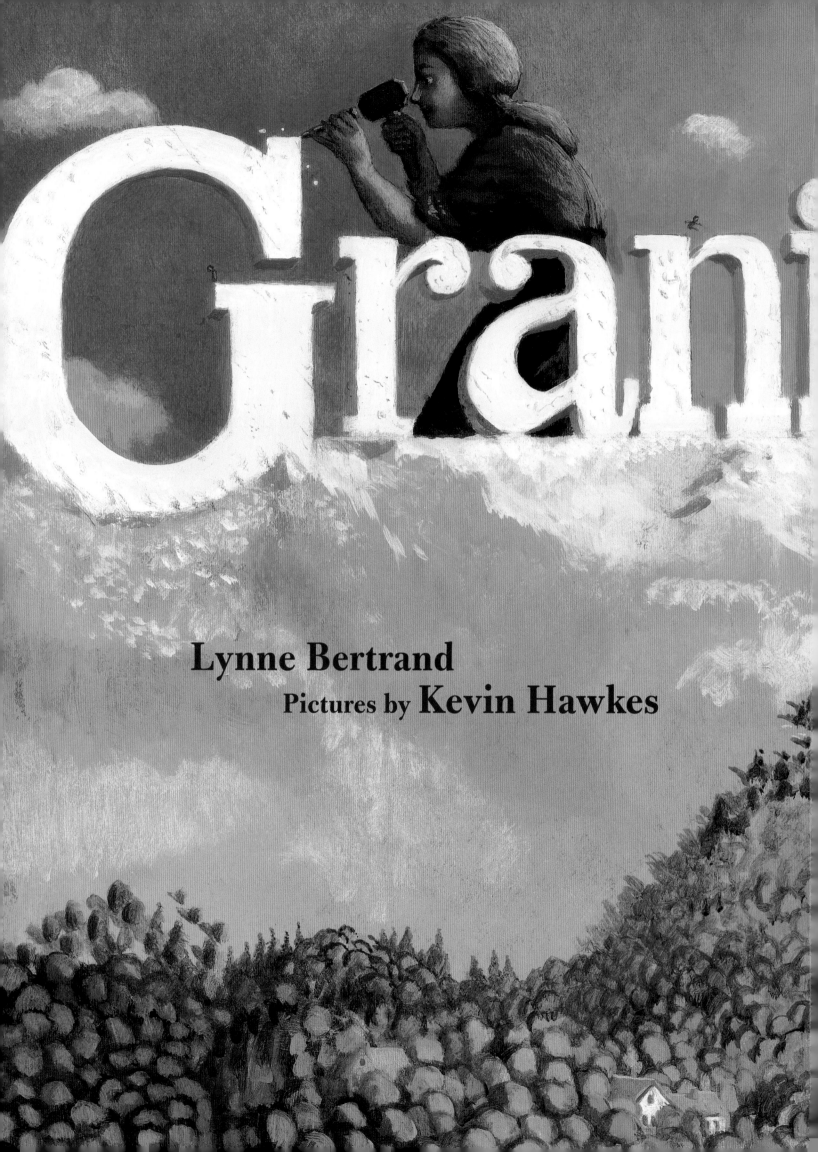

Grani

Lynne Bertrand
Pictures by Kevin Hawkes

te Baby

Melanie Kroupa Books
Farrar, Straus and Giroux
New York

Back in the time when folks first discovered granite deep under the north woods of New Hampshire, five burly sisters opened a stone quarry up on Umbagog Lake. They filled their camp with picks, drills, and ropes, and harnessed a team of northern blackflies to pull their stone wagon.

Each of the sisters had a special talent. Jade could twist the river like a rag in her hands. Em whittled wood. Golda was handy with string. People said Ruby was half bear, she was that strong. And Beryl was the finest stonecutter in the Granite State. No mountain was too big for Beryl.

In fact, no problem was too big for any of the sisters. But there came a day when they faced a problem that was, you might say, too small.

It all began one day at high noon, when Beryl carved up a mouth-watering picnic for her sisters. She carved granite root beer and finger sandwiches, granite dip and deviled eggs. She carved granite napkins and even a hound dog out of granite to devour the leftovers. That old stone dog was so real-looking he peed on the picnic blanket and buried a ham bone.

Beryl was duly pleased with herself, but her sisters said, "Do go on!" And as Beryl was not one to shy from a challenge, she did.

She quarried a fresh pit from an outcrop of rock, blocked it, and carved it into a brand-new town, right down to granite pillows on every bed and a curl of granite smoke rising from every chimney.

"Oh, my," said the sisters. "Do go on!"

"All right," said Beryl, feeling mighty pleased with herself. "See that bit of pink granite over there? That one at the foot of Kinsman Mountain? Watch as I carve it into a real live baby."

And she did.

The sisters named him Lil Fella, and he was as dear as any backwoods baby—if a mite heavier than most.

They loved him right away. But a minute didn't pass before all five sisters realized they had no experience at all with such a small thing as a baby.

From afternoon till midnight, and midnight till dawn, Lil Fella cried, wailed, screamed, and hollered till you could actually see his yellin' in the crisp New Hampshire air. It looked like a dark cloud of alphabet letters, pitchin' and buckin' and pokin' everybody so that pretty soon nobody north of the Kancamagus Highway could eat, sleep, or plow.

Folks in Vermont shot a look of disapproval at the five sisters. They called across the river, "Why don't you do something for that poor little baby?"

"What'll we do?" said the sisters.

Now, there was one person watching all this hurly-burly with interest,
and that was Nellie, a backwoods girl from up to Franconia Notch who came
to marvel at the sisters' work. She hoped to be a stonecutter herself one day.
Although Nellie was so small she could barely lift a chisel, she knew a bit
about babies. Back home, she had two dozen or so little brothers and sisters
trailing her everywhere.

"Pardon me!" she yelled, loud as she could to be heard over Lil Fella's caterwaul.

"Shhh!" whispered the sisters. "Can't you see there's a baby here!"

Nellie whispered back, "Pardon me. But I wonder if maybe that baby's crying 'cause he's cold."

"Well," said Sister Beryl, "I'll warm him up." Then she took her pick from behind her ear and carved a granite layette for that baby, of speckled gray riding boots and top hats, smoking jackets and bow ties. She carved button-up gloves and monogrammed handkerchiefs, embroidered vests and argyle socks, all out of stone.

When you laid them all out together, those clothes were heavier than a
ship's anchor, but they looked as fine as a page out of the Sears, Roebuck catalog.

"There, that'll do," said Sister Beryl.

But did that baby quit crying?

No, ma'am. He balled up his little fists and kept right on. The Vermonters
over the river rolled their eyes.

"Maybe that baby needs to be fed," said Nellie.

"Fed?" said Sister Jade. "Were we supposed to feed him?" She lifted the mighty Connecticut River in her hands and twisted it into a silver knot and rubbed it till it boiled.

She threw in a ton of roast beef, fourteen hundred sacks of Maine potatoes, a pile of cabbages higher than Pikes Peak, and half an onion. The steam of that boiled dinner filled the entire north woods like a gamey fog.

"There, that'll do," Jade said.

But did Lil Fella stop crying?

Uh-uh. He squeezed his eyes shut and wailed.

"Maybe that baby wants to be rocked," Nellie said.

So Em went to work whittling a first-rate rocking chair. The raw piece of maple lumber alone weighed three ounces more than the whole state of Vermont. On it, Em carved more flowers than God himself planted in the Garden of Eden. The two maple runners required 324 gallons of beeswax. The wax cloud started its own clover-honey-smelling weather system, which drifted north to Canada, where it made the English language stick in people's throats and come out sounding like French.

The finished chair required a full day to rock forward and another day
to rock back.

"There, that'll do," said Em. She set Lil Fella in the rocker and gave it
a push.

But did he stop crying?

Not hardly. In fact, his color ran to beet purple and his yellin' turned to
all capital letters.

"Maybe," said Nellie, "a small plaything would cheer that baby."
Sister Golda grabbed her string and, with a slip of her burly fingers, fashioned a covered bridge for Lil Fella, with string fisher-cats and mountain lions racing back and forth between her fingers. On the rail of that bridge she wove a string telescope so Lil Fella could view a pod of string whales breaching off Cape Cod.

And at five minutes to six, a string engine and seventy-two cars of the Boston & Maine blew south on the rail, hooting whistles, chugging black smoke, and running on schedule for the first time since pine trees were sticky.

"There, that'll do," said Golda.

But did Lil Fella stop crying?

"No" is right. He wrinkled up his face like a piece of old apple and kept on.

"That baby might be bothered by the bright sun," said Nellie.
Sister Ruby drew herself up and said, "Well, I'll get him some shade."
Ruby shoved her fingers under Dixville Notch and picked up the entire
White Mountain divide and shook it out like a hallway carpet till all the
peaks flapped in the sky, and dirt, trees, and wild things rained down on
New England.

Deer Mountain landed just so, and cast a soft shadow over Lil Fella's eyes, but Ruby wasn't done yet. She reached around to the other side of the earth, dragged the moon over the horizon, and shoved that in front of the sun, too, bringing on a full solar eclipse. Cold, black dark fell on the north country like a box trap on a jackrabbit.

"There, that'll do," said Ruby.

Did Lil Fella quit wailing now?

No, not by half.

Folks in Vermont were starting to investigate whether they could move their whole state over to the other side of Maine just to get some quiet, not to mention some desirable Atlantic coastline in the bargain.

But people in Maine said, "Don't bother coming—we can hear Lil Fella's yellin' over here, clear's a bell."

So the five sisters all turned to Nellie. "What'll we do?"

"Here," said Nellie. "I'll do it." And she took Lil Fella into her arms.
She shifted him gently onto her hip and said, in her smallest and kindest
voice, "Hello, Sweet Pea. Hello there." She poured him a small bottle of warm
milk. She cleaned him up and wrapped him in a small, soft blanket. Then she
sat down on the front porch, and they watched the backwoods children
running with the bluetick hounds.

Lil Fella unclenched his fists. He opened his squeezed-shut eyes. His color returned to a soft, peachy pink. Then that baby grinned a milky grin and fell asleep.

"There," said Nellie, gently cuddling Lil Fella in her arms. "That'll do."

The silence, which nobody north of the Kancamagus Highway had heard since the day Lil Fella came to be carved, sounded like this:

All over the north woods, folks were so confounded relieved they raised a silent toast in honor of Nellie, while Lil Fella slept peacefully all afternoon. But at sundown, that baby's howls once again filled the northern sky. Babies cry at sundown, that's a fact.

This time, the sisters knew what to do. Sister Beryl carved a tiny rattle that fit just right in Lil Fella's tiny hand. Jade gave him a small, warm Umbagog bath. Golda rigged up a cozy little string cradle. And Em whittled a bowl of oatmeal so lovely and small that it looked to belong to—well, a baby. Lil Fella was satisfied with just that much.

But as the bright sun eased down between the White Mountains and shone right into Lil Fella's eyes, it caused one last fuss. Sister Ruby, who could move mountains and drag the moon across the north sky when she needed to, just smiled at that baby—

and gently turned his cradle around.

For Papa, the Nickster, Ms. G, J.T.S., and C.M.J.
With thanks to Fran and Linda Judd, stone quarriers —L.B.

For Mason —K.H.

Text copyright © 2005 by Lynne Bertrand
Illustrations copyright © 2005 by Kevin Hawkes
All rights reserved
Distributed in Canada by Douglas & McIntyre Ltd.
Color separations by Chroma Graphics PTE Ltd.
Designed by Barbara Grzeslo
First edition, 2005
Printed in October 2010 in China by Kwong Fat Offset Printing,
Dao Jiao District, Dongguan City
5 7 9 10 8 6 4

www.fsgkidsbooks.com

Library of Congress Cataloging-in-Publication Data
Bertrand, Lynne.
    Granite baby / by Lynne Bertrand ; pictures by Kevin Hawkes.—
1st ed.
        p. cm.
    Summary: Five talented New Hampshire sisters try to care for a baby
that one of them has carved out of granite.
    ISBN: 978-0-374-32761-3
    [1. Babies—Fiction. 2. New Hampshire—Fiction. 3. Tall tales.]
I. Hawkes, Kevin, ill. II. Title.

PZ7.B46358Gr 2005
[E]—dc21
                                                    2002192882

(Canada)

Vermont

New Ha